THE GREAT FARM ADVENTURE

DHRISHIT SHAH

INDIA • SINGAPORE • MALAYSIA

ISBN 979-8-89067-980-2

Contents

Chapter 1

A Journey – and a Puzzle

"These holidays have been the dullest ones we've ever had," said Hardik, to his brother Gaurav, a boy of nine and sister Aanya, a girl of thirteen. They all nodded. They all had an awful cough and cold along with high fever and were in bed for the whole of their holidays. Now only two weeks were left and there was a faint hope in their minds that the doctor would allow doorbell rang and the doctor arrived.

"Hello children," said the doctor. "Hope you all are feeling good." "Doctor, their temperature is normal, their cold is also gone. But they still cough a lot." "Well, to get rid of their coughs, you should take them somewhere where the air is not polluted. A farm, for instance." Hardik, Gaurav and Aanya immediately cheered up and set up an awful fit of coughing. "Thank you doctor. We will surely think about it," said mother.

"Mother, please search for a good farm where we can enjoy the rest of the holidays," requested Hardik, as soon as the doctor went. "We'll talk about it in the night when father comes," said mother. A whole day's wait was a long wait for them. When father came, they began their discussion. However, father said, "I have to go to Kashmir for a business trip and would like mother to join me. I won't take you all as even in summer, it will be snowing heavily. I have had a talk with my sister to come here and I can't send you alone to an unknown place."

At once there were cries of dismay.

"Oh father, please don't say no."

"Oh father, Hardik is of fourteen. He can take care of us."

"But father, the doctor advised us to go to a farm."

However, father was firm in his decision. Suddenly Hardik brightened up. "Father, I know a farm where you wouldn't mind to send us alone. It is Wellington Farm. You remember George Wellington, my school friend, don't you? His parents bought a big farmhouse in the middle of a vast farm in the outskirts of Mumbai. We can stay there, can't we? Oh father, please call George and ask him." "Not a bad idea, I'll call him," said father.

Everyone waited as father called him. Much to their delight, they heard him saying, "Oh great. When can we come? Yes, that will suit us very well. Thank you." Father hung the call and said, "We will be going tomorrow so better start packing. I will drop you by car. We will leave at sharp half past ten and will reach by twelve."

They shouted in glee, only to find themselves start coughing. They began to pack and were discussing about

George. “What is he like?” asked Gaurav. “You will find him very funny,” said Hardik with a grin. “He came from America and was new at our school.”

Mother came in at that moment and exclaimed that in such a cold winter, they had not packed any warm clothes and decided to do their herself. “Go and play,” she said. They found it very difficult to pass the whole day.

Finally, tomorrow came. Hardik was the first one to wake up and looked out of the window. He was pleased to find it bright and sunny. He awoke the others. They got ready and were waiting for the car.

“Mother, have you packed the binoculars?” asked Aanya, who was very fond of gazing at birds. “No,” replied mother. “Pack it.”

The car came and hooted so loudly and they almost jumped out of skins. “There was no need to hoot so loudly,” said mother, crossly. The luggage was put in the boot and they started. The first part of the journey was very boring. It was the same view which they saw everyday – tall buildings; noisy, honking vehicles; polluted air; large and small shops; shouting hawkers; chattering people.

Seeing that everyone was bored, Hardik took this opportunity to tell more about George.

“George is one of the most interesting people in the world. He is master in everything, except Hindi. He is good and trustworthy – he never tells lies but he is very mischievous.

He has his pockets full of all kinds of prank things. If he gives you any wrapped gift in the middle of our stay, then open it with your head away from it." "Why?" asked the others, including father. "Because there may be a punching hand attached to a spring which may be attached to the bottom of the gift. As soon as you open the gift, it will come out with full force." "Um, I don't approve of such tricks," said father. "It may hurt the person." "Father, I agree that this trick isn't very good, but there is another wonderful trick of him. I don't know from where, but he gets such water balloons which when blown look exactly like a fruit. Then he will not allow you to touch it (as you will come to know it isn't a fruit) and will ask you to cut it. When the unsuspecting person will try to cut it, it will burst and water will get squirted on the person," grinned Hardik.

"Don't his parents scold him?" asked Gaurav, remembering the scolding his parents had given him when he once tricked his sister Aanya. "Yes, they did scold him but knowing that it wouldn't matter they cut on his favorite things like chocolates," said Hardik.

"I'm surprised that the teachers didn't remove him from school for some days," said Aanya. Hardik grinned and said, "George is mischievous but he is truthful and extremely witty too. That's why everyone likes him, even the teachers. Only Aarav doesn't like him. Since our classrooms had no CCTV CAMERAS, it was very difficult to find out who did mischief. Taking advantage of this, he hatched a full proof plan to trap George. Before the first period, when we had to go to the auditorium for a meeting, he pretended to be searching his notebook. So, when he was alone, he did something with the teacher's chair. After the meeting, when our class teacher sat on it, it broke and he fell. He was very angry and asked who did it. So, Aarav said that it must be George as he was the only one who did mischief. But George intelligently said that it wasn't him and he also added that there was a hidden CCTV CAMERA and he could find out through that. The teacher understood his plan and added that the one who is caught through it will get double punishment. So, Aarav confessed that he did it to trap George."

Everyone laughed.

"But then didn't he reveal that there was no hidden camera?" asked Gaurav. "No," said Hardik. Gaurav asked, "But why?" Before Hardik could answer, Aanya answered, "Use your brains, silly. If he didn't reveal, then everyone would fear of getting caught by the hidden camera and no one would dare to do any mischief. Right?" Hardik nodded.

"Now children, please look out at the greenery," said father. "You won't see any in Mumbai." The children looked out of the window.

It was certainly a beautiful sight.

On each side of the road were many plants. Some were short, some were tall; some had green leaves, some had brown – red leaves; some had fruits, some had flowers, some had none. In the middle, thorny rose bushes grew, blooming hundreds of sweet-scented roses. All around the rose bushes, taller chili plants grew. There were very few chilies, indicating that the chilies were recently picked. All around the chili plants grew pink chrysanthemum flowers. Then, in the border grew plants of onions, potatoes, aloe vera and bananas. Beautiful birds were feeding on fruits.

Aanya was about to remove her binoculars but Gaurav let out such a loud shout that all the birds flew away in fright. "I am hungry," he yelled. "Gaurav," scolded Aanya crossly. "Just when the view is perfect and the birds are still, you have to shout." Gaurav again shouted a repeated what he said before, taking no notice of Aanya's remarks.

"There are so many bananas in the trees. You can easily pluck them," said father, jokingly. But Gaurav took it so seriously that when he saw a banana

within his reach, he opened the window and plucked it. He was about to fall but Hardik caught him and pulled him in the car.

"Gaurav, can't you sit quietly in the car and enjoy the views outside?" asked father, exasperated, while Gaurav happily ate his banana

Now the view had changed to dry, barren land. There was soil all round, only in some places bushes grew. Farmers could be seen working – some were sowing seeds, some were carrying water, some were adjusting machinery, some were discussing and some were making a list of something.

Soon the road forked into three. There was a signboard which showed: “George said A Farms,” said Hardik.

So, they went straight. Soon they came across many farms, identified by numbers. “George said Farm No.5,” said Hardik. They all got out of the car and went to farm 5. The gate was open and they went in. There was a woman, milking the cows, with a scowl on her face. “She must be the helper and George must have tricked her,” thought Hardik. She saw them asked who they were. “Good afternoon ma’am,” said father. “We have come to stay here. George Wellington, the son of the owners has invited us.”

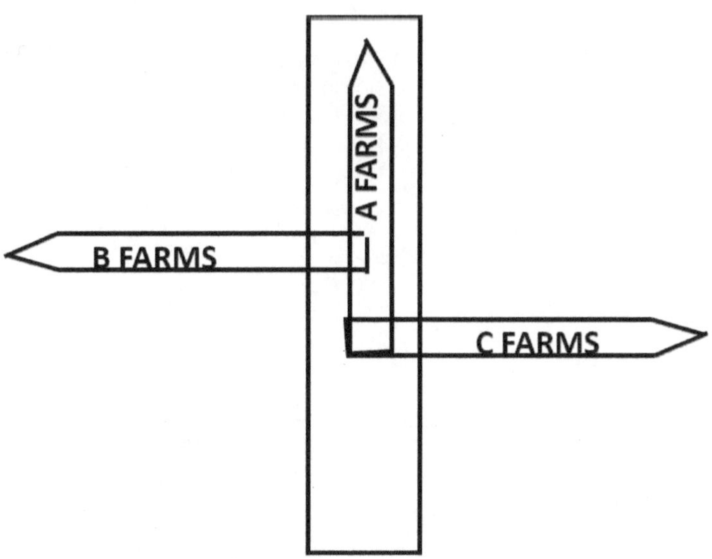

But to their enormous surprise, instead of welcoming them, the woman shouted at them, “No George stays here. If you think that it is funny entering into people’s houses, then I'll call the police." They all were speechless. Father asked, "Isn't it Farm A No.5?" However, the woman said that it was Farm B No.5. "Can't even see the signboard," she grumbled and went away. They all went to the car and drove back to the signboard. To their enormous surprise, it showed entirely different. It indeed was a puzzle.

Chapter 2

The Changing Signboard

"This doesn't make any sense," said father. "Someone has fiddled with the signboard, I'm sure of this. But why would someone do such a silly thing?" "Maybe the fiddler finds it funny to misguide people and waste their time," said Gaurav.

"Maybe," said father. "Now, do we follow the signboard or take left, assuming that the signboard is again wrong?"

"Follow the signboard," said the three children in a chorus. Father was about to start the car but Hardik shouted. "Wait. I think I saw George hiding in that bush. Same spiky hair, same slim body. But it can't be him." "Yes, it can't be him," said father. Again, father was about to start the car but Gaurav stopped him. "Can't we call George and ask him left or right?" "Yes," said father and immediately called him. However, he didn't pick the call.

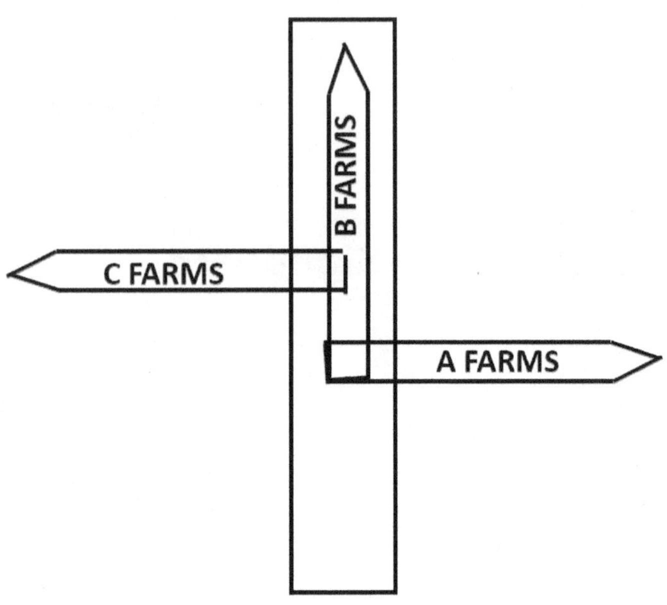

Without any further delay, they took right. Then they again came to farm 5 and went there.

A man was there, feeding the farm animals. As soon as they entered, the dogs set up a terrific row of barking. The man came there and asked, “Who are you all,” with a surly look on his face. “Good afternoon sir,” said father. “We have come to stay here. George Wellington, the son of the owners has invited us.” The man said, “That George stays in A Farms. Go there. This is C Farms,” and went away.

When they sat in the car and went to the signboard, it had changed again. “Now it showed correct – A Farms to the left, B Farms straight and C Farms to the right,” said

Aánya. "But after wasting half an hour – it is half past twelve," added father.

They went to the left and saw Farm 5. On reaching there, they saw a woman reading a book. On seeing them, she greeted. "Are you all lost and want shelter? Come in. Lunch is ready." They were taken aback.

"Isn't this Farm 5?" asked father. "Because outside it says so." But before the woman could say no, George came.

"Hello everyone. Why are you all here? My farm is the next one." Everyone was relieved to see George. Hardik said, "Outside it showed that this was Farm 5 and yours was Farm 6.

So, we came here." George seemed to be surprised. He took us out and to our utmost surprise, George was right. But Aanya's sharp eyes saw something which they didn't see. She saw some gum on the wooden sign which showed the farm numbers.

"Someone must have stuck the wrong numbers with gum to fool us and then removed it but some glue was left," said Aanya.

The others nodded. However, George started laughing. He said, "That someone is me. Yes, I just wanted to give you all a grand welcome so –" "So you changed the signboard every time and made us go the wrong way and when we came left, you made us go to the wrong farm, right?" asked Hardik and George nodded. He said, "I came to the signboard much before you came. The directions were fixed to it with the help of screws, so I just got a screwdriver, loosened them and changed them."

"So, it was you indeed hiding in the bush, when I saw you. And that is why you didn't pick up our call. It is a pity we don't have your parents' number in father's phone," said Hardik.

They all laughed but father was indignant. "I don't approve to fiddle with any public property," he said. "And before you go, take your luggage out of the car. I have to leave," he added. They took their luggage and carried it to the farm.

Mrs Wellington came out and said, "Oh, you all are here at last. I asked your mother and she said that you all left pretty early. And George, where were you? You went out at half past eleven and it is one o' clock." Everyone grinned. However, George, being truthful told her what he had been doing that delayed them so much.

"I was laughing so much," he said at the end and began laughing again. "George," she said crossly. "Show them the farmhouse."

George at once took them inside the farmhouse and showed the hall. It was a big one, with four cozy sofas, a huge television, a large empty space for playing and many things like pictures, fancy lights and fans, etc for design.

They entered the kitchen and stared in awe. It was huge. There was a storeroom too, and a dry area for washing machine. They then saw two bedrooms. "They are for mother and father," he said. Now I'll show your rooms and they climbed the staircase. There were two guest rooms. The one in which they were going to sleep was very spacious. It had a huge king-sized bed. "We all are going to sleep," said George. "Here is the bathroom if you all want to freshen up a bit. Do it fast because lunch will be served soon."

They all freshened up and came to the dining table. There was tomato soup, broccoli soup, salad, mayonnaise sandwiches, cheese corn balls, different types of paneer and potato curry, cheese macaroni, roti and vegetable pizza. In the desert was plum pie, chocolate cake and rasgullas.

At once there came cries of astonishment.

"Whew, what a spread. I can't decide what to start with."

"Wow, such delicious dishes. You are a wonderful cook, aunt."

When lunch was over, not a single dish was left. "Now what do you propose to do, George?" asked Hardik. George said, "I thought of showing you all the farm. At the corner of the farm there is a small two-storey house, called Wellington Hut, also called as Wellington Cottage, more like a cottage, where all the farm helpers stayed. But now they all are off for a week's holiday. Today is Monday, so they will return on Friday. Till then we manage the farm. So, I can show you everything after the unpacking is done. We'll do that first."

"Right," said Aanya.

They all went up and removed their bags. "It's an awful bore to remove the same things you put yesterday," said Hardik, and George and Gaurav nodded. But Aanya didn't. "Don't you remember that mother did our packing, and George can also help you if you feel like."

George grinned and gave them a hand. He was surprised at what they brought. "Why do you need jackets in a hot summer like this," he asked. "And why did you all bring stationery?"

But a last, the unpacking was done and everything was neatly arranged in cupboards. "Now you all can go down and explore the farm," said Mrs Wellington. So, they all went down, ready to explore the farm.

Chapter 3

Wellington Farm

George said, "We'll walk around the farm and I will show you everything. Then we can go to the cottage and explore it."

"But you said that the house was for farm helpers, so will they mind if we explore it?" asked Gaurav.

"Oh yes. I told you that they were out and took all their belongings. It is empty now. Let's walk around the farm."

While walking, they first came across a board which showed 'VEGETABLES'. George said, "Behind the farmhouse, we grow some vegetables. Around it is grass where we walk, drive tractors, etc. This bush," and pointed to the rightmost one, "is where carrots grow. There are some already. The next one grows tomatoes and the leftmost one grows peas. We grow very less vegetables, flowers and fruits."

Aanya asked, "Where do you but other things from?"

"There is a shop nearby at a walking distance which sells practically everything replied George. "Now let's continue walking."

They walked and came to the left of the farmhouse. There were no plants, but soil only. George said, "This part is yet to be cultivated. When the helpers return, we will plant broccoli, chili, and cauliflower. Towards the end to it is the machine shed where we keep all the tools. From the machinery shed, if you look straight, you can see the cottage. The others looked at the shed and then at the cottage. They nodded.

"It is such a wonderful farm," said Gaurav, pronouncing the word 'wonderful' incorrectly. George grinned. Then he suddenly looked surprised.

I say," he said. "Look, there is a fresh tomato on the soil." The others looked down and nodded. Aanya picked it up doubtfully. As soon as she picked it up, she realized that it was a water balloon Hardik was talking about in the car. But before she could throw it down, George, as quick as lightning took a pin out of his pocket and burst in and all the water fell on poor Aanya.

Aanya's face went red with anger and she darted for George. But clever George ran quickly towards the flower farm to the right of the farmhouse and Aanya forgot all her anger on seeing the sight. "Come here," she said to Hardik and Gaurav.

It was indeed a welcoming sight. All kinds of flowers grew and it was almost impossible to differentiate between them.

George said, "Actually we were going to separate the flowers the same way we separated the vegetables but while the seeds were being sown, I had played the water balloon prank on one of my friends so he chased me all the way and while running, I mistakenly bumped into father who had all the seeds and all of them fell in the soil. That's why all flowers are growing randomly."

The others laughed. "I bet you got an awful telling off," said Hardik. "In the starting I got, but when the flowers grew, it looked so beautiful that I was praised," said George, grinning. Gaurav said, "It does look beautiful. Sunflowers, with many hibiscuses covered with a layer of roses and many other unknown flowers." The others agreed. Now they walked to the front of the farmhouse and saw grass for vehicles and people.

George said, “Now, what do you want to see first? The other farms and the general store or the cottage?” Hardik said, “I think that we’ll see the other farms and then have a look at the general store. My pen’s ink is over and I have to do my vacation homework. Does it sell pens?”

George replied yes and then they all went out of the farm. They were looking at all the farms from outside. One farm had so many vegetables laden on trees that they could open a vegetable shop. “That’s farm 8. It is called the ‘Vegetable Farm’ due to abundance of vegetables. Sometimes if we need vegetables urgently, then we buy it from this farm.”

They all then saw that the farms ended and there were many shops. “Electronic Shop, Stationery Shop, Toys Shop, Cloth Shop, Nursery, Restaurants, Salon,” read out Gaurav. “B and C Farms also have the same shops,” said George.

"But if there are so many shops, then what does the general store sell," asked Aanya. George replied, "Everything apart from what these shops sell. For e.g. it sells grains, pulses, idols, furniture, etc."

Gaurav said, "It must be a very big shop then." "Yes, it is. That's why it is called ABC SHOP. The name of the area is ABC FARMS." Hardik asked, "Can't I buy a pen from the stationery shop then?" However, George shook his head and said that their pens get over very quickly."

The road soon turned right and it merged with two more roads. There they saw the general store. "This road merges with the B and C Farm roads," explained George and the others nodded. They went to the store and saw a plump old woman there, smiling all over her face. "Hello George," she said. "Who are they?" George replied, "They are my friends. I was showing them ABC Farms." Hardik asked, "Do you have this pen's refill?" The woman saw the pen and gave him the refill. He paid and they were about to go but the woman suddenly stopped them.

"Wait," she said. "I just remembered something. Dr. Demon is caught and imprisoned." The others were blank but George squealed in delight. "Oh, this is great news. Thanks a lot for telling this." Now seeing that the others were blank, George said, "Dr. Demon's real name is Dr. Abhishek, but everyone calls him Dr. Demon. He was a scientist and was working with other scientists to invent such a battery that would convert a small amount of solar energy into a huge amount of electricity. While doing so, they mistakenly invented something that, when exposed to hydrogen, could blast a huge area. So, Dr. Demon stole it and hid it somewhere in Wellington Farm in a special bag and escaped. So, from that day, which was a week ago, a policeman comes with a device and scans the whole farm, hoping to detect it. They completed scanning Wellington Hut and Wellington Farmhouse. Now they will scan Wellington Farm."

"But that chemical is very dangerous and can blast huge area," said Hardik. George nodded and continued, "Dr. Abhishek has a remote which when pressed, can open the bag in which the chemical is there. He hopes to escape prison and leave the Country. Then he will open the bag and blast this area." Everyone was horrified. "It is said that Dr. Demon gave that remote to his wife and sister, who are roaming freely in the country," said George, who was enjoying the look of their faces.

"Come on, let's go to the farm and explore Wellington Hut," said Hardik, voicing the thoughts of the other two. They all went all the way back to the farm. But before they could explore the cottage, Mrs Wellington came out and said, "George, we have got two people here this night and I have to do a lot of cooking. They will set up tents on the camping place and I want you to help me do the household work I don't know when they will go. Show them your games and they will play." However, much to Hardik's and Gaurav's dismay, Aanya suggested that they should also help her. Mrs Wellington was pleased.

She asked George and Gaurav to sweep up the camping place and then water the vegetables, as they always did it in the evening. She asked Hardik to sweep up the hall, Aanya to help her in the kitchen and then both would water the plants.

They all set off but they were stopped as the aroma of the delicious food entered their nose. They were ravenous and wanted a good meal.

They munched every sandwich, ate every samosa, gobbled every piece of cake and drank every drop of lemonade. After the wonderful meal, they were ready to do any work Mrs Wellington told.

Mrs Wellington and Aanya completed the kitchen work quickly. Mrs Wellington did the cooking while Aanya handed her all the ingredients and did little things like washing and drying utensils. Then, Aanya asked her about Dr. Demon if she knew more. However, she told the same things that George told but one thing she heard made her keep her eyes wide.

Aanya heard, “The night when the scientist came to the farm, I heard digging and drilling sounds but I thought that that was one of the farm men. Later, when I knew it, I examined every inch of the farm but didn’t find any place where there was grass before and it disappeared, or the ground was hard and became soft.

Then I remembered that the workers had gone to their home that night so she checked the cottage as well but found no sign of anything being dug. Unfortunately, Mr. Wellington has been out since a month and I am unable to contact him."

They continued cooking and completed it. Aanya saw that Hardik as going very slow so she watered the flowers herself.

Meanwhile, Hardik was going very slowly as he was relating this story to the book he had read. In it, it told that a man did a robbery and hid it in an underground tunnel which he made from his house to a playground. Hardik was thinking if Dr. Demon also made a tunnel in the farm.

Soon he also completed and went to see Aanya.

Meanwhile, George and Gaurav were sweeping the camping place and around it. They were also discussing something, but not about Dr. Demon. Instead they were thinking of tricks to fool Hardik and Aanya.

Gaurav suddenly started laughing and told his plan to George, who grinned from one ear to the another. "That is a fantastic plan, Gaurav. And I always carry water balloons in my pocket. But have you thought anything about Dr. Demon?" Gaurav shook his head. George continued, "I have thought a little."

He said, "If Dr. Demon did some kind of robbery that he could sell and earn a lot of money, then he wouldn't tell his friends where he hid as they would sell and become rich. But in this case, Dr. Demon wants to blast this area so he would be most happy to tell his friends where the chemical is kept so they can do the work. So, if a policeman disguises himself and takes him out of the prison, Dr. Demon would tell him where it was kept and then the police would arrest him again and then take out the chemical."

Gaurav asked, "But why would he tell where the chemical is kept?" "Because if he gets caught again, then someone will know the secret and blast this area, silly," said George. Soon they completed sweeping and watering and ran to meet the others. They were waiting for them to pour out their ideas. Soon there was such a pandemonium that they had to cover their ears.

"Everyone tell one by one," said Hardik.

Aanya told everyone how Mrs Wellington heard digging and drilling but found no change in the farm ground or in the cottage.

Then Hardik told his idea of an underground tunnel which could link somewhere to the farm. He also guessed that Dr. Demon must have drilled from somewhere to right under the farm and hid the chemicals. The others thought for a second and thought that is was very likely to happen. But then the question was how to find the tunnel?

The answer to this question was George's idea. He immediately poured it out and the others stared at him in awe. How intelligent he was to think of it. "But then we will have to convince the police," said Aanya, looking doubtful. "Oh, that's easy," said George. "The police knows me all right. We'll go to the police station and tell our idea. But first we'll ask mum."

They went to the farm and before they could take permission, Mrs Wellington said, "The police will be here in an hour to scan the farm. If you want to explore the cottage, then better do it now." The others nodded. They went to the cottage but its door was locked. George removed the keys from his pocket and unlocked the big, stout wooden door and turned the lights on.

Chapter 4

Wellington Hut

"Look. Here there are two tables where the helpers have their meals. There are four helpers in total. One for cleaning the farmhouse, one for cleaning the farm, one for gardening and one for doing the household work. There were chairs here but they are in the farmhouse as no one stays here. Come, we will climb the staircase and I will show you the top floor," said George.

"Wait," said Hardik. "Isn't this a television?" "Oh yes. I forgot to tell you that. This television is used by helpers mainly for news. They like to know the conditions of the state their family lives in. And we always allow their family to come here and stay for somedays in the farmhouse. And we give them a fifteen-day holiday either in the month of November, or December if they want to go to their house."

"Wow, that's great on your part," said Aanya and they all agreed. They climbed the staircase and found two bedrooms with a king-sized bed and two small beds to accommodate two adults in each room. They entered the left room.

There was a bathroom, quite small but easily manageable. A grand king-sized bed reminded them of their beds, which were in their rooms in the farmhouse. They suddenly yawned and then grinned. "Whenever I yawn, my mother thinks I am sleepy and I am sent to bed," said George, grinning. "Good thing she isn't here."

The others nodded. There was a large wooden cupboard and next to it were two windows, from where daylight made its way into the room. There was a curtain above the bed, closing a window. A round clock above it was still working. It was all very grand but one thing puzzled them a lot. There was a real plant next to the bed. “It is a lemon plant, yet to be planted in the farm. The police strictly told us to make no change and the plant was given by my friend, who arrived yesterday. So, we will plant it when the police allows us to,” said George. The others nodded.

They now left the room and entered the other room. There was again a small bathroom, but quite manageable. There were two single beds with a night lamp on each side. Above the beds were two portraits, set up on a blue wall, instead of a brown one. There was a small balcony in this room with three plants. The curtains also had leaf shaped designs. It was evident that one of the two men who lived in the room was the gardener.

"Isn't there a cupboard?" asked Hardik. "No," replied George. "The gardener and the household helper, who live here, want a plain vertical wooden piece with racks in it. They prefer the things open, so there is no door in it. To put big things, the use the ladder and put them on the top."

The others stared in astonishment. "It is very good of you to give the helpers a good place to live. Otherwise nowadays people don't care about their workers," said Aanya, who was very sensitive towards people. "Come on, now let's go back to the farmhouse," said George. "Or else mum will be worrying."

They all climbed down the main staircase and went out. George carefully locked the door. While going, they saw two men setting up tents in the camping area. George approached them. "Hello sir. Are you the ones whom we expected now?" "Yes," replied one. He, like the other, was a short, fat person with an ugly face. He could easily be identified with his bright rid eyebrows and the other with his bright blue hair. "They look like clowns," whispered Gaurav to Hardik, who shushed him.

They walked to the farmhouse. However, on opening the door, a bucket full of water fell on Aanya.

She immediately looked at George furiously, who grinned and said, “I saw a nail hammered in the wall for a portrait and used it for a bucket instead. I filled it with water, took a big stool and put it on it, such that the top of the door was exactly in level with the bottom of the bucket. So, when Aanya opened the door, the top of the door pushed the bottom of the bucket, the bucket tilted and the water in it fell on Aanya.” Aanya was about to pick up a fight with George put the door opened and two policemen came with a strange device in their hand. “Call your Mother, George,” said one and George did so.

In a moment Mrs Wellington came and requested the police to have dinner first and then do the scanning. “Just what we thought, ma’am,” said one of them and the other grinned. As they were going, the two men came and asked, “Ma’am, is the dinner ready?” and were surprised to see police at the table. Without waiting for a response, the fled back to their tents.

“Who were those, George? And who are these children?” asked one inspector. George replied, “Those men are camping at our farm, sir. And he is Hardik, my school friend. He has come to stay here with his brother Gaurav and sister Aanya. They had got an awful cough and the doctor suggested them to go to a farm so they are staying here. And he is Inspector Aryan and he is inspector Karan.”

"Girl, why are you wet?" asked Inspector Karan. He was a tall, well-built man with dark skin and a pleasant face. Aanya immediately went red. "George's trick, I suppose," said Inspector Aryan, grinning. He was a tall, slim man with fair skin and a grinning face.

Aanya nodded. Mrs Wellington came in at that moment with a lot of dishes and cutlery. The boys went to help her, while Aanya went up to dry herself and change. She realized that their window pointed towards the tents and she could see the men. "I wonder why they ran on seeing the police. Have they committed some crime and now, to escape have come to a farm? I'm sure they're up to no good," she thought.

She suddenly remembered her binoculars and decided to spy on them. On seeing through them, her mouth fell open and she gasped. They were removing their bright red moustache and their hair. She realized that the moustache was fake and the other man wore a wig. But if the man had healthy black hair which she saw after the wig was removed, then why should he wear a wig?

She heard her name being called and immediately rushed down, looking excited. There were thoughts racing in her mind. "Have I discovered something very important? Will the inspectors be happy on hearing this? Oh dear, what will the others say, especially George. It was because of his prank that I saw the men's real face."

Chapter 5

A Fine Dinner – and a Scan

"Where were you, Aanya?" asked Hardik, cross. "Mrs Wellington refused to give dinner till you came. "Actually I –" said Aanya and stopped. She was about to tell them what she saw, but thought, "It isn't necessary that they are criminals. They might just wear the wig and moustache for fashion and if they, then the police will doubt them and they might even leave the farm in anger." She was just thinking but George asked, "You were saying

something?" Aanya replied, "Um yes. I just slipped and my ankle was aching so I took rest. But now it's fine. My word, what a spread!"

It indeed was a wonderful spread. Baby corn soup, onion soup, green salad, slices of baby potatoes, white, red and pink sauce pasta, tawa pulao, roti, onion curry, paneer curry and pickle. In the dessert was jalebi, gulab jamun and chocolate cake. "Wow Mrs Wellington. You really have mastered Indian dishes," said Inspector Karan and Inspector Aryan nodded. However, the children were too busy in completing their food and taking more to say anything.

When dinner was completed, George rushed to their room and came out with three gifts with a label of the children's names. Hardik and Aanya were doubtful but Gaurav opened it and found a watch. Seeing the gift, Hardik and Aanya relaxed and immediately opened their gifts but to their surprise and shock, a punching hand attached to a spring came out of Hardik's gift and gave him a good punch on the nose. And in Aanya's gift, a dozen of water balloons attached to a spring and flew out and burst on poor Aanya's face, making her wet again.

They both went red with anger. "Wetting me the third time. I've a good mind to complain to the police," said fierce Aanya, of course. "And may I know the reason of sparing Gaurav?" asked Hardik, in a polite tone full of anger. Gaurav grinned. "While sweeping the farm, I gave George this idea. And this is Gaurav's watch only." Mrs Wellington came in at that moment to take the dishes. "Why Aanya, you are all wet again. And Hardik, what has happened to your nose?" she exclaimed and then turned to George, suspecting him. But George only grinned. "I think we should start the scan," said Inspector Aryan, bored but amused. They all nodded and went out, except poor Aanya, who went up to change. Again, she looked out of the window and saw those two campers, but this time with their fake moustache and wig.

She went down and joined the police. Inspector Aryan said, "We'll look at the grass first," and they went towards the gate. They started the machine and a bright green light was emitted. "How does this machine work?" asked

Hardik. Inspector Aryan said, "The chemical Dr. Abhishek hid is a dangerous acid. You must have learnt that acids are reactive and this acid reacts with hydrogen, as you know. So, this machine detects acids and on detecting this light turns red and we hear a beep beep sound."

"But how does it detect acids," asked Hardik. "We're policemen, not scientists," said Inspector Aryan with a grin. Then they went a little further and away from the gate and to their delight, they machine light turned red and a beep beep sound came. Inspector Karan said, "We've found the chemical. Quickly get the spades. We've got to dig here." In a thrice the children ran to the machine shed and got some tools.

Hardik and George were carrying two spades each, one for them and one for a policeman. Aanya and Gaurav were carrying one spade each for them. They started digging. However, the ground was very hard and they found it very difficult to dig. "Get some water, everyone," said Inspector Karan and all, including the inspectors went and filled a bucket full of water. Soon the soil became soft and porous and gave the way as they again started to dig with the sharp spades.

They all worked hard and suddenly, when George hit something with his spade that gave a sound which sounded like a metallic clink. Everyone gathered around it and began to dig there. They soon came across a glass jar with a yellow liquid. George said, "It is an acid which starts from S but I don't remember its name. It increases the soil's nitrates and we use it once in a blue moon. But since there was no space as we were renovating the farmhouse, we stored it here and then forgot all about it. I'll give it to mum." And he ran to the farmhouse, leaving everyone dejected. "I think we can scan tomorrow, as it is dark," said Hardik and the children nodded. However, Inspector Aryan said, "We are police. We always work in the night. Anyways, this green light is enough. Now let's fill up this hole."

George came and grinned on seeing everyone busy filling up the hole. He gave them a hand and the hole was filled. They again started scanning and came to the tents. The two men came out and Inspector Karan asked, "Would you mind if we scanned the ground of your tents." One man said, "Yes, we do mind. We won't allow anyone, let be a policeman to scan our things. Now clear off, or we'll complain about you and you all will be demoted from inspector to sergeant," and both went inside.

"Funny men they are. Perhaps they think it is some silly joke," said Inspector Karan. They didn't scan near the tents but went to the grassy part to the left of the farmhouse. After a quarter of an hour, the light turned red, but this time very bright and the beep beep sound was very loud. Inspector Aryan and Inspector Karan were too pleased for words. "We've found it. It is a very strong acid so it is beeping so loudly," they exclaimed in delight.

The children ran to the spot where they previously dug and got all the tools. They ran and came back and started digging. They dug such a big hole that Gaurav needed help to come out. Inspector Aryan and Inspector Karan switched their torches on and helped Gaurav come out. Soon, they found a very disappointing thing. Again, there was the same acid in glass jars which helped become soil nutrient-rich. However, there were dozens of jars this time, so the machine was beeping so loudly.

"Have to ask Master Wellington where more have they stored this acid," said Inspector Aryan. George came running to them, grinning. "Mum promised me not to punish me for any mischief tomorrow," he said. But before Inspector Aryan could say something, Gaurav asked, "Are there more jars of this acid?" George shook his head.

"Now let's get started again," said Inspector Karan and they began to fill up the hole. It was such a big hole that it took a large amount of time to complete the work and then they continued their scanning. However, they found nothing in the grassy land. They then heeded towards the vegetable farm. In the way, they crossed the farmhouse and saw the two men having their dinner.

"If those men are busy having their dinner, then we can scan the ground of the tents," said Gaurav and Inspector Aryan agreed as well as Inspector Karan agreed. They quietly went to their tents and scanned the ground. However, nothing was found.

"Let's go to the vegetable farm," said Inspector Karan and they went. Although everyone was going slowly, Aanya was way behind them. "Buck up Aanya," said Hardik. "Do you want to miss the fun?" However, Aanya turned a deaf ear towards him and continued looking at what happened to be the farmhouse window. The others also noticed that and Inspector Karan asked, "What happened, girl? Anything wrong with the window?"

Aanya replied, "The two men are constantly looking at us as if they want to know what we are doing. I think that there is something fishy with them. Don't you remember how they fled on seeing the police. And when I went up to change, I didn't slip but I saw them removing their *wig* and *fake moustache*. I thought it to be fashion for them but I'm not sure now. And they didn't allow us to enter their tents. And now, they are spying on us."

"Hmm", said both the inspectors and then looked at each other and nodded. The others were puzzled. "What happened sir," asked Hardik. Inspector Aryan replied, "Keep an eye on them. Many times, it has happened that people commit some crime, escape to some quiet place and once the hue and cry is died, disguise themselves and stay." The others nodded.

"But is there any way to find out if they are escaped criminals?" asked George. Inspector Karan said, "Read every newspaper you have at your farmhouse, even if it is a year old. There may be news of robbery or some other crime." The others nodded. "We'll surely do that tomorrow, sir," said Hardik and they started walking again.

"Here are the vegetables," said George and the policemen scanned but nothing was found. "Now to the flower farm," said Inspector Karan. While going from the vegetable farm to the flower farm, they had to cross the tents. As soon as the men saw them, they closed the flap of the tent which acted like a door. "Keep an eye on them," repeated Inspector Aryan.

They came to the flower farm. "What a beauty!" exclaimed both the inspectors. George grinned. They scanned the flower farm too, but found nothing. "I think that Dr. Abhishek hid the chemical somewhere else and came cleverly came here to misguide us," said Inspector Karan and Inspector Aryan nodded.

They went to the farmhouse to tell Mrs. Wellington what they thought. However, she said, "I told you that I heard drilling and digging sounds in the night." But, Inspector Karan said, "That was to put us on the wrong track. Dr. Abhishek was found on a dry, barren land near the farms. Other policemen are scanning that and we hope to trace it there. I'll came them right away and tell them that we have failed to find it here."

But before he could call them, they called him. They heard inspector Karan say, "Even we have failed. I think that the chemical is hidden somewhere else," and cut the phone.

George grinned and said, "I had thought of an idea this evening. We could easily know the location of the chemical."

But Inspector Karan shushed him and said, “There is no time for jokes, Master Wellington. This is serious.” But ignoring the response, George poured out his idea and the two inspectors grinned.

Chapter 6

A Smashing Surprise

"That's a nice idea, I must admit, but the problem is that Dr. Demon is very clever. He will easily understand that it is our plan and he will tell us a wrong place and set us on a wild goose chase," said Inspector Aryan, and Inspector Karan nodded.

"Come on, now let's go back to the farmhouse. I want to know from Mrs Wellington about those men," said Inspector Karan and they started walking. However, as they reached the farmhouse, the men were having their dessert.

"Have the mango ice-cream, I just made it," said Mrs Wellington. "Inspector Karan was about to ask her what they wanted to know nut Inspector Aryan whispered, "The men are here and we don't want them to get suspicious. We'll eat the ice-cream and then, when they go, we'll ask."

So, everyone nodded and began to eat it. It was so yummy that Inspector Karan asked for a second helping and the children asked for a third. As they completed their ice-cream, the men went back to their tents.

When Mrs Wellington came to take the dishes, Inspector Aryan asked, "Ma'am, can we know something about those two men. We feel

suspicious about the." But Mrs Wellington said, "Oh, they're all right. The one with the moustache is called Soham and the one with red hair is called Pratham. They live in a small flat in Dadar."

"Ok, thank you for the information, ma'am," said Inspector Aryan. "We'll leave now." And saying this, they went away.

"Funny they are, aren't they," said Mrs Wellington to the children, after the two policemen were safely out of the farm. The children nodded. "Policemen are always like that, mum," said George.

"Now go to bed, all of you. It is ten o' clock," said Mrs Wellington. "Don't forget that you all have a cough." But George said, "They haven't even coughed once. We'll play Uno for sometime." Mrs Wellington nodded.

They all changed into night suits one by one. George went first as the others didn't mind. However, he took a lot of time but soon came out and winked at Gaurav, but the other two didn't notice.

Soon, all four were in bed, playing Uno. Aanya's luck was the worst, unlike Gaurav, who yelled Uno the first and won in his next turn.

This was a good excuse for Gaurav to tease his fierce little sister, who in anger, thumped her head on her pillow, and to her enormous surprise, the pillow burst and water came out, making her and the bed all wet.

"George!" she yelled at the top of her voice and immediately darted towards him, while George ran around the room, followed by an angry girl.

Mrs Wellington came to tell them to stop playing and sleep, but she was surprised to find George chased by an angry wet Aanya.

"George," said Mrs Wellington in distress. "If this is one of your pranks on poor Aanya, making her wet for the fourth time, then no dessert for you tomorrow. And everyone please go to sleep. And Aanya, please change." But before George could plead her, she went and Aanya grinned. "Serves you right, Master Wellington," she said annoyingly. She changed outside and everyone went to sleep, except for poor Aanya, who checked her pillow, mattress, blanket and what not. "They're real," she said to herself and went to sleep.

Everyone slept like logs. No one stirred when the whistle of the cooker came piercing through the air, or not even when Mrs Wellington came in their room to take a heavy recipe book and mistakenly dropped with a thud.

George was the first one to wake up, for he wasn't ill, unlike the other children two days before.

He looked out of the window and was pleased to find it nice and sunny. He also saw the tents and the two men,

Soham and Pratham were out. But he could see properly, for they were far. So, he took the binoculars and saw them without their red moustache and wig.

“They ought to be careful,” thought George. “Removing their fake things outside the tents and getting scared on seeing the police, anyone would guess that something was fishy. Hardik, who was sleeping beside him awoke by the sudden movement.

“What are you seeing through the binoculars,” he asked. George put the binoculars in front of Hardik’s eyes and he saw what George was seeing. “Aha,” he said. “So Aanya was saying the truth.”

Gaurav and Aanya awoke at the very moment and Hardik was glad that Aanya didn’t hear that. Aanya said, “I got a very good sleep on the wet bed. I dreamt that I was sleeping in a pool. Good think aunt didn’t notice the bed wet.”

George immediately said, “Like me to play another trick on you this night?” Aanya hurriedly said, “No thanks. I’ll manage.” George grinned, “I was joking. Now let’s get ready and go down to the dining table.” Everyone got ready and went down.

Mrs Wellington greeted them. “Good morning. Had a good sleep, I hope.” Everyone nodded. George asked, “Have the campers had their breakfast?” Mrs Wellington said, “Oh yes. When I got up, I saw them reading a book. They completed the breakfast as soon I made it. Now they’re out, exploring this area.”

Everyone was surprised. "How do they wake up so early," asked Gaurav, remembering how much he troubled his mother in the morning. "You ask them when they come," said Mrs Wellington, laughing. "I'll get the breakfast." Hardik said, "We'll help," and the others nodded. They went in the kitchen and exclaimed, "Whoa! Dhokla, khandvi, masala idli with milk."

They were soon eating and drinking milk, telling Mrs Wellington now and then how tasty the food was. She laughed. "You enjoy the food," she said. When breakfast was finished, Aanya offered to help Mrs Wellington with the dishes. "The boys will be no good at that, except for breaking things," said Aanya, teasingly.

Mrs Wellington was pleased. She and Aanya were busy in the kitchen, while the boys thought of completing their vacation homework. George and Hardik had to solve extremely difficult equations, while Gaurav had to write a small essay on 'trees' and do general grammar.

"Lucky," said George and Hardik to Gaurav, while they were busy scratching their heads and trying to simplify the equation. Aanya came out and grinned at their hard work. "Good thing I did mine immediately after school," she said. Gaurav completed his very quickly but Hardik and George took loads of time. But at last, they completed too.

"Now what should we do?" asked Gaurav. George said, "We could play hide-n-seek, couldn't we?"

Hardik thought for a moment and asked, "Where?" George replied, "The whole farm excluding the machine shed and the top floor of the farmhouse. We can hide in the ground floor."

Everyone thought that it was a great idea. "Right," said Aanya. "Whoever wants to be the denner will be ahead of the others." But much to her anger and annoyance, the boys stepped behind. George said, "You are ahead, so you are the denner." "All right," said Aanya, gruffly and she began the countdown from hundred.

Hardik took the keys from George, rushed to Wellington Hut, unlocked the door, climbed the staircase, entered the right room. He climbed the ladder, and lay still on the top of the door-less cupboard. "Aanya may climb the staircase, but will search in the cupboard in the left room," he thought.

George rushed to the farmhouse, went in the kitchen and hid I side the storeroom. He turned the light on and was surprised but pleased to find his favourite chocolate there. "So that's where mum hides it when I do some mischief," he said to himself and started eating it.

Meanwhile, Gaurav was hiding somewhere where he wasn't allowed to. He was hiding outside the gate of Wellington farm. He thought that when Aanya would be tired of hunting for him, he would secretly enter the farm and show himself.

Aanya was thinking where to find everyone. She suddenly remembered the storeroom in the kitchen of the farmhouse – that would be a great hiding place. She went in the kitchen and heard some sound in the storeroom. She opened the door only to find George, devouring dozens of chocolates.

She then went inside the cottage, climbed the staircase and entered the left room, but no one was there. So, she entered the right room and saw that no one was there. She was about to leave but saw the ladder and climbed it to find Hardik.

She then searched everything to find Gaurav but couldn't find him. But, how could she? For Gaurav was doing cheating. Gaurav was laughing to himself and was about to enter the farm but he saw the two campers, Soham and Pratham, talking to a camper in Farm 6.

"Must be their friend," he thought and then showed himself. They continued playing till Mrs Wellington came in the farm after doing some shopping. But beside her was a dog! Everyone was astonished. "Maybe aunt wants to make it a proper farm with animals," suggested Hardik.

On looking at their surprised faces, Mrs Wellington smiled and said, "While coming, I saw it on the road, hurt. So, I took it to Mr. Vinod of Farm 4, who is a vet. From then, it isn't leaving me." The others appreciated her for her deed and the dog immediately ran towards them.

It was a small, brown, chihuahua with a white tail. The children left their game and started playing with it.

George asked, "Are we going to keep it forever? For we need animals to make it a proper farm."

But Mrs Wellington said, "No, we can't. Mr. Vinod read in the newspaper that this dog is missing and the person who finds it has to call a number. So, when we called, the receiver said that he was out and the dog ran from its caretaker. So, till he comes, we can keep it. Its name is Fluffy."

The children nodded and continued playing with Fluffy, and Mrs Wellington went in the house. George too went in the house and came out with a bright red ball. He threw it in the air and Fluffy immediately caught it by its mouth.

The next two hours were spent in throwing all kinds of balls, dry twigs and soft toys, and Fluffy leaping and catching it. "He would make a perfect fielder in cricket," said Gaurav and everyone nodded. "But the thing is that he would catch the ball before it reached the batsman," said Hardik and the others laughed.

Chapter 7

A Search – and a Big Blunder

Mrs Wellington came out and said, "Children, lunch us ready. You'd better come in and have it while it is hot." The children nodded and ran in to wash their hands. Fluffy, also ran behind them and sat under the dinner table.

"Woof," he barked.

"Give him some biscuits, George," said Mrs Wellington and George gave Fluffy a bowl full of them and left him munching. The children sat on the

lunch table and exclaimed, "Whoa! Why do people in farms make so much food, unlike people in cities, where there is only one item."

There was tomato soup, broccoli soup, green salad, freshly cut vegetable sandwiches, fried rice, dal, roti, paneer curry, vegetable curry and spinach spaghetti.

George didn't even start eating but asked, "What's for dessert? Something special, I'm sure." Mrs Wellington said, "Your favourite American style chocolate brownie and your favourite Indian rasmalai." George immediately scream with joy but Mrs Wellington asked, “Forgot last night’s wet happenings and sweet punishment?”

George immediately sulked and started eating his food. But he couldn’t sulk long as the scrumptious food didn’t allow him and was soon joking and laughing with everyone.

But when dessert was placed, Mrs Wellington smiled and put in his plate also. He was overjoyed. Mrs Wellington said, “For this time only,” and went in the kitchen. “Now I’ll have my meal,” she said.

Everyone nodded and went in their room, while Fluffy the dog went to the doormat and slept. “Now what do we do,” asked Aanya. Gaurav said, “Play some game, maybe Uno.” But George shook his head and said, “Look at the newspapers, as the two inspectors said. We keep all the newspapers in the storeroom.”

Everyone agreed. George went downstairs and in the storeroom. He looked at the bundles – there were five of them. He called everyone downstairs, but together they could carry only one.

“We’ll first check this bundle, then take the others one by one. I possibly can’t carry another, even with the help of all, including mum,” said George, as they went in their room. “Same here,” said everyone.

So, they all were busy flipping the pages of every newspaper and looking at them in case they found anything that would please the police. But nothing interesting was found.

However, George and Gaurav found it very funny and interesting.

"Joker fired by circus head for making the watchers laugh more," they read out loud, making Hardik and Aanya get irritated. "And look at this," said Gaurav and George read with a very funny laugh that fascinated Gaurav, "Kidnapper kidnaps man and asks for his water bottle in ransom."

"Can you two just be quiet for a moment?" asked Hardik, annoyed. "The kidnapped man must have hidden something precious in the bottle and the kidnapper came to know from somewhere." "Yes," said Aanya. "You all aren't searching for what we want, you all are searching for silly things. I'll get some water and come." And saying this, she went down.

"Hey, look here," said George and the two looked at what he was pointing. It was two years ago when Dr. Abhishek had got the best scientist award for technology and inventions.

"So, two years ago, he was good," said Hardik, but Gaurav shook his head.

He pointed to another newspaper that was a year ago – and the same news was printed on it. Hardik said, "So, if Dr. Demon, or rather Dr. Abhishek was so famous, then why should he commit a crime? Because being so popular, he can be spotted by many people who know him."

The other two nodded.

"Maybe because he didn't get the award this year," said Gaurav. But before he could get a reply, Aanya came up with a jug of water and asked, "Found something interesting?" The three showed her what they saw and she nodded.

But before she could say anything, Gaurav pulled out a newspaper from the bundle and the whole bundle fell on poor Aanya's legs. Disbalanced, Aanya fell on the bed and the jug of water in her hand fell on the newspaper Gaurav had pulled.

Gaurav immediately backed away and shaked the paper up and down violently, sending millions of tiny water droplets. "What are you doing?" he asked Aanya angrily. But Aanya also replied the same thing. "What are you doing? Making all the papers fall," she said.

But Gaurav said nothing and showed them a photo in the newspaper. "It's Dr. Demon!" exclaimed the others. Gaurav nodded and showed them the text next to it. "Aanya spilled water on it, so now it's unreadable. It might have something very important, which might give us some clue about him," he said.

"Let's try to read the text, just in case we can," said Aanya, who was anxious to reverse her blunder. Gaurav nodded and tried to read but couldn't. "No use," he said. "A lot of water fell on it by our honourable careful Aanya." This was said sarcastically, of course.

Aanya went red with anger. Hardik saw this and said, "Let's continue." All nodded and again started. After about ten minutes, they found something interesting. In a paper it was written – 'Yesterday a man rushed to our newspaper printing house and gives a photo of some scientist, along with something written and asks to publish in the paper. The next day, before delivering the paper, all except one get stolen by the same scientist whose article was published in the paper. The delivery person realises that the last paper can get stolen, so gives it to his school friend, who he finds near and tells us everything. The school friend, on reading this paper, please come at our printing house and return yesterday's paper, it may contain something important.'

"Aha," said George. "My father told me that he had a very close school friend, Uncle Jim. He then migrated to India and –"

"And this newspaper is nine days before. That means the man spied on the scientist ten days ago. That means –" screamed Gaurav.

"That means that the scientist is Dr. Demon, because he stole the chemical seven days ago. So, –" said Hardik.

"So, that information must be related to Dr. Demon's plan of stealing the chemical, so that the scientists must be careful about the chemical's security," said George.

"But the information is no more readable now," said Aanya, mournfully. "But why didn't you all return the paper? And didn't you all read the information in the paper?"

George said, "We were not at home the day the paper came. And father didn't want to read an old paper. And the funny thing is, he didn't find anything suspicious when he saw uncle's face."

"But didn't you all read the information in the paper?" asked Aanya again. George said, "My father must have forgotten to read that very page. Everything wrong for us and right for Dr. Demon." Everyone but Hardik agreed with the last line of George. "What happened Hardik?" asked Gaurav. "Are you thinking something?"

Hardik still didn't reply. It was only after Gaurav shouted, Hardik heard him. He said, "Um yes. Listen to this. Dr. Demon was found in this farm and the barren land last week's night. However, nothing was found on scanning. So, can it be that he wrapped something around the acid's bag that is not allowing it to be detected?"

Gaurav asked, "How it is possible?" "He's a scientist," said Hardik. He looked at the others and the nodded. "Can be," said George. "After all, the acid didn't blast because the bag doesn't allow hydrogen to pass through it or the acid to leak. And we guess that the acid or the machine release some waves which detects the acid. So, the bag may not allow the waves to pass through it."

Hardik and Aanya nodded but Gaurav was blank. "I don't understand all this," he said. "All I understand is that I'm hungry." The others realised that they were hungry too. "It is five hours since we had lunch and I'm ravenous. I'm sure mum will have something good," said George. "We'll continue scanning these papers later."

So, they all rushed down, only to find Mrs Wellington come up. “Oh, I was going to call you all for snacks, but it is good that you all remembered,” she said. Everyone nodded and rushed to the dining table. “Fluffy is still sleeping, I meant to play with him,” said Aanya.

As they saw the dishes, they were elated. “French fries, homemade potato chips, burgers and my favourite rasmalai in dessert. Superb!” exclaimed George. Gaurav complimented, “Aunt, you are a super chef.” Mrs Wellington laughed and went in the kitchen.

As soon as the snacks were over, Fluffy woke up, much to the delight of Aanya and disappointment of the other three. “We could have completed our work,” said Hardik. But Gaurav grinned and said, “It’s ok. We can do the work without Aanya.”

Hardik nodded and they both went up, except George, who went in another room. He came out very quickly with a green ball and told Aanya, “Play with this.” He then threw the ball towards Aanya, said “Catch it,” and ran up at top speed.

Aanya was puzzled at George’s sudden run, but didn’t think much and caught the ball over her head as it was too highly thrown. However, to her amazement and anger, the ball burst and water fell on her, wetting her from head to toe. Fluffy was thirsty, and on seeing water, began to lick Aanya. “George,” she shouted and raced up, while Fluffy went in the kitchen to ask for water.

Meanwhile, George was narrating everyone his latest water balloon prank, making the other two laugh till their stomach ached. However, on seeing Aanya at the doorstep, they both hid behind the bed.

However, George, not scared of anyone or anything, asked her, "Had a good bath?" On hearing this, the two hidden boys chuckled, but Aanya replied, "Oh yes, it was fun. And I've come here to give you some fun." And saying this, she showed George a tumbler full of water.

George shrieked and ran around the room, followed by a wet Aanya, chasing him with a wet tumbler. However, while running, George suddenly stopped and pushed the tumbler towards Aanya before she could even lift it, wetting her for the sixth time.

On seeing this, Hardik and Gaurav couldn't help laughing, but a glare from the fierce Aanya was enough to stop and quieten them. "Next time I will chase you both with a tumbler," she said. "And I will again empty the tumbler on you," grinned George, only to find himself pushed on the floor by Aanya.

Mrs Wellington came up at that moment with Fluffy to tell them to play with him, but was surprised on seeing Aanya all wet again. "Oh dear, I suppose it is George the fifth time," she said in distress. "I need to punish him."

Aanya said, "Sixth time, aunt, not fifth time. First wetting me with his horrible water balloons, and the emptying the tumbler I bought on me only." Mrs Wellington screamed,

"Sixth time! No dinner for you, George. Only bread and butter, without dessert. And one more punishment, come down and help me in the kitchen, while they play with Fluffy."

And saying this, Mrs Wellington went away, followed by a pleading George, leaving Aanya grinning from ear to ear and the others horrified.

"Serves him right," said Aanya as she went out to change. Hardik and Gaurav were quietly scanning the papers, and it took a long amount of time without George and Aanya.

Aanya, determined to punish all the boys, left them to do the work and herself played with Fluffy.

She thought to herself, "Fluffy is my best friend. Not like George, who always targets me for his next prank, not like Gaurav, who leaves no opportunity to tease or trouble me, and not like Hardik, who never listens to us, as we are smaller than him."

Chapter 8

A Day Full of Mischeif – and a Movie

Finally, George completed helping in the kitchen, the two boys scanned all the papers but found nothing, and Fluffy, tired, went to his mat and slept.

Very fortunately for George, at dinner time, Aanya's temper had died down and she was laughing and enjoying the food with the others. But poor George had to eat plain bread, and wasn't even allowed to eat butter. The others were puzzled, and asked why. Mrs Wellington replied, "I had planned tomato soup, but while bringing tomatoes, he slipped and all the tomatoes fell on his face and got wasted."

Everyone laughed. Mrs Wellington said, "Then I planned broccoli soup, but while bringing them, he saw a cockroach and in fright, threw all of them and they landed outside the farmhouse through the window." Again, everyone laughed.

George went red but Mrs Wellington continued, "Then, I prepared to make dal makhni, but while it was in the cooker, I had to go to the washroom, so I told him to turn the gas off after two whistles, but George waited for me to whistle and ignored the cooker's whistle. So, by the time I came back, it was all black."

Again, everyone laughed. Mrs Wellington then said, "I realised that George can never cook, so I sent him out and made all myself. But I could only make salad, roti, paneer curry and dal rice." The others grinned and looked at George, who wasn't enjoying this at all.

After dinner, much to the amazement of everyone, they felt sleepy. "Then go to sleep. After all, you all were ill with cough and cold for so many days, and now you are recovering." Everyone nodded and went to bed.

The next day, everyone were awake at seven. "Looks like our cold is gone," said Aanya and everyone nodded. They got ready very quickly and at half past seven, were down at the breakfast table.

George was horrified to see two plates of bread butter on the table. "I am not going to eat this today at any cost, even if I have to stay hungry," he said stubbornly and fiercely. Mrs Wellington laughed and said, "These are for the campers, they are visiting Mumbai and will eat bread butter for lunch."

Just as she completed speaking, the two men came, as sulky as ever. "And with their fake moustache and wig," thought Aanya as Mrs Wellington packed the bread butter and handed over to them. Without a word of thanks, they went away.

The children's eyes fell on the food and squealed with delight. "Dosa, dhokla, mango shake, and milk for anyone who wanted it. But who would want plain milk when mango shake is available," exclaimed the children. Mrs Wellington laughed as she went out.

Gaurav asked, "Aunt, who waters the plants when the gardener is on leave?" Mrs Wellington said, "I do it," and went out to do the same. But Hardik said, "Aunt, we will do it after breakfast. You please rest."

Everyone nodded, Mrs Wellington smiled and Fluffy barked from under the table.

After breakfast, George led them to the garden hose. "It is so long that I can water the vegetables of Farm 6 with it," he boasted as the other three stared at it in awe. George uncoiled the hose with Gaurav's help and was taken to the flower farm by Hardik and Aanya.

"I'm turning it on," said George, but to his utmost dismay, the tap wouldn't move. "It's jammed," he said and no matter how hard he or the others tried, it wouldn't move. So, the children called Mrs Wellington for help but it was of no use. Even she couldn't.

"It's ok. We will fill water from the bathroom in tumblers and then water the plants," said Hardik, and George gave them each a tumbler.

However, much to Aanya's surprise, by the time she reached the flowers, her tumbler was half empty always.

"It doesn't drain outside," she said, and to her relief, water didn't disappear in her fourth fill. But, when the watering was completed, George pulled out a pin from his pocket and pierced it in Aanya's tumbler. Immediately, it burst and a lot of water fell on Aanya.

George grinned and said, "This is a special air balloon, which has a hole in it. The water in it used to flow in it and get trapped inside it. So, when I burst it, the water in it fell on Aanya."

Aanya stared at George in horror, her eyes blazing red. "Now no one can save you from me. Fluffy is asleep, so you cannot use him to make me happy." And saying this, she darted towards George.

George ran towards the farmhouse door and stopped in front of it. When Aanya came extremely near him, he opened the door and ran inside the house. But from somewhere, a bucket full of water fell on Aanya, drenching her from head to toe.

But before she could explode, Mrs Wellington came out on hearing the noise, and was amazed to see Aanya completely wet. She immediately understood that George was behind all this. "George! What punishment do I give you?" she thundered and then suddenly her eyes twinkled and said, "Do the shopping for me today." And saying this, she gave him a note which showed all the things to get. Aanya grinned and went up to change, while poor George had to go to the market.

"Whenever George tricks Aanya, he gets a punishment and Aanya plays on her own, leaving us bored," said Hardik to Gaurav, once all three were safely out of sight.

Gaurav nodded and said, "Yes, but it is fun to see what new trick George is going to play, for he has endless tricks. But now, what do we do?" Hardik said, "Play with Fluffy."

And before he could even complete, Fluffy came towards them, his tongue as wet as ever. But he didn't stop, he was searching the whole farm and then again went inside the farmhouse. "To find Aanya, perhaps," said Gaurav and Hardik nodded. "Now that Aanya is angry, she will not allow us to play with Fluffy. So, what do we do now?" asked Hardik and Gaurav sighed. "Nothing," he said. "Wait for George."

So, the two boys sat by the flower farm, sometimes admiring the beauty and sometimes complaining about the fact that they were getting crushed between George's tricks and Aanya's anger.

At last George came, grinning all over his face, as if nothing had happened half an hour before. Hardik was angry with him, but Gaurav ran to him and asked, "What happened? Why are you so happy?" George said, "My water balloons were about to get over, but I spotted Vihaan in the market and he gave me lots of them."

Gaurav asked, "Who is Vihaan and why did he give you water balloons?"

George replied, "Vihaan is a genius – he makes these balloons himself. But he doesn't want to reveal his secret formula, and that's why he gives these balloons to some trusted friends only. But he doesn't tell how he makes them."

Gaurav called Hardik loudly, and was immediately shushed by George. "Don't tell this to anyone, silly. Only mum and dad know this," he said in a fierce whisper.

Aanya suddenly appeared in front of George with Fluffy and said, "I have a challenge for you. I will give you a high catch and you won't be able to catch it." George grinned, "Throw the ball."

Aanya threw a bright blue ball and George caught it easily. "Now you catch," he said and threw the ball to Hardik, who was approaching them. Hardik caught it above his head, and it burst over him. A lot of water fell on him, and he was half angry, half puzzled.

"So that's why Fluffy did not run towards it. But why didn't this horrible water balloon burst on you?" he asked. George grinned and said, "There is a technique to catch it in such a way that it doesn't burst. And I used the same technique."

Hardik decided not to be angry with him, so he laughed and told Aanya, "You are very lucky that George didn't target you, although you targeted him. I'll be back in a minute," and went in the farmhouse to change.

Aanya went in the green patches of the farmhouse with Fluffy, and was soon playing with it.

Gaurav told George, "This water balloon prank is getting very old. I doubt if they will even fall for it. Why don't we plan something new?" George nodded and said, "Let's think of some new trick. But we'll play it on both after lunch."

Hardik came down with a pack of Uno cards and asked, "Want to play?" The two nodded and asked Aanya, who shook her head. So, till lunch time, the three boys played Uno, while Aanya enjoyed with Fluffy.

As soon as lunch was served, the children ran to the table with an exclamation with delight. "Baby corn soup, salad, cheese corn balls, noodles, roti, potato curry, mix veg curry, and in dessert there is brownie."

The children enjoyed the lunch immensely. And after they completed, Mrs Wellington said, "We are going to watch the movie – 'THE CHASE' right now on computer.

Everyone was pleased. George said, "I wanted to see it since a month, but couldn't as mum was busy." However, to his shock, Mrs Wellington said, "You are not seeing the movie. You can see it only if you don't do any mischief till a month. And nobody will dare to tell him anything about the movie."

George immediately sulked and went away, while the others enjoyed the movie. But as soon as the movie was over, he came running to them with a small piece of paper.

"I found it in our cottage, stuck to a wall on the ground floor," he said.

"What were you doing there?" asked Hardik. George said, "To water the lemon plant which my friend had given. But when I saw the note, I forgot to water it."

Everyone, even Fluffy poured over the note.

> 28670830 9306685 494 4 028475930 595993 488499968 93774 99493 03876903 5993920 0385
>
> 249008320 2993489584 200874890 29988885
>
> 5945264969 632929 8574590485945 78720114
>
> 039848 40493839
>
> A.S

"Whatever does that mean?" asked Aanya. George said, "Look down silly. A.S. means Abhishek Singh."

"Who is he?" asked Gaurav, puzzled even more. George said, "Dr. Demon. His full name is Abhishek Singh."

"But how do you know?" asked Gaurav, still puzzled. With a tone of disgust, George asked, "Then whose note can it be in our cottage, especially after the theft of the chemical? He must have left it for his wife and sister after hiding it."

Hardik nodded. "George is right. These words must be some code, whose solution his partners, or whoever they are, have. But the funny thing is that neither we nor the police noticed it stuck on the wall.

George turned the paper and they saw that the paper's design and the wall's design were similar. "Maybe his partner also couldn't spot it as it is camouflaged so nicely," he said.

Hardik clapped George on the back and said, "Well done. I'll call both the inspectors right away. They'll be pleased with you."

However, much to his surprise, George screamed, "No!" Hardik asked, "Why? Is it a prank? Because the ink on this note is still wet, as if recently written."

George knew that he was caught, and ran away at top speed.

Chapter 9

A Puzzling Thing

At snacks time, the children got a horrid shock. There was a note attached to the dining table which read –

Dear George,

Your father has suffered a severe leg fracture, hence I had to leave for Delhi. I have asked Mrs Sharma of farm 8 to give you all the meals, and please take care of everyone. It is a good thing that Fluffy is with you all, so he can protect you from thieves.

Your mom.

George was aghast. "I knew that this kind of thing would happen while we were trying to solve a mystery," he said, while he was being comforted by all.

Fluffy, sensing that something was upsetting them, licked George's hand and he felt better. "Let's go and take our food," he said.

But before they could go, Mrs Sharma came and gave them some bread jam, and bread butter. She patted George. "I'm sorry about this, but everything will get better," she said.

George smiled as she went away, and they ate their food. The whole evening was spent in playing Uno, and George, for the first time, felt as if he didn't want to trick anyone. So, to make him feel better, they purposely played bad and made George win.

In dinner was roti and paneer curry. "I know I can't make meals which your mom made, but I'm trying my best," said Mrs Sharma.

After dinner, George wanted to go to bed, so everyone went. No one heard the telephone ring at its loudest, the two campers pick it up, talk in George's voice to Inspector Aryan and take important information from him.

At midnight, George suddenly woke up, no knowing why. Then he realised that he was thirsty, so he went in the kitchen. However, he saw a light in Wellington Hut.

"Can it be the two campers, taking advantage of mom's absence?" he thought. Then he smiled. "In the school play, I was a ghost. I will wear those masks and scare them to death."

So, George went in his room, took the mask, and was about to leave, but Gaurav woke up. On hearing the story, he too wore a mask, and the two set off.

As they reached the cottage, they went near a window and immediately popped up, scaring the two people in the hut. But to their enormous surprise, a sharp woman voice spoke, "Shut up, Soham Pratham. You only had to dress like a ghost, not scare like one. Take this note and remember Wellington Hut, ground floor."

The two boys were dumbfounded.

They quietly took the note and ran back to their beds, welcomed by an excited Fluffy. The excitement was too much for them. George put the note in his pocket and went to sleep, and had dreams where ghosts gave him strange notes. He woke up at 7 o' clock with a jump, and thanked that they were only dreams. He woke everyone up, and they got ready. Mrs Sharma said, "I have made khandvi, bread jam and bread butter. Hope the khandvi good." The children complimented a lot, much to the relief of Mrs Sharma.

As soon as she went, George and Gaurav narrated their midnight experience and showed the note. But, the other two just laughed. "George and Gaurav again up some mischief, I suppose," said Hardik. "Plus, wasn't the hut scanned?" "Woof," said Fluffy, as if he was agreeing with him. Aanya immediately gave him biscuits, and he got quiet.

Gaurav then spoke, "Why would we do this note prank the second time, when we know that it won't work?"

Hardik said, "So that we think the same and believe you." Gaurav was about to say something, but George stopped him and said, "Leave it. Let them not believe us if they don't want to. But we will live in Wellington Hut by ourselves and solve the mystery."

Gaurav nodded and completed their breakfast. He then whistled to Fluffy as if he was calling him, but Fluffy went to Aanya and sat down. Aanya laughed. “There, Fluffy also knows that you all are fibbing.”

The two said nothing, but packed all their things in Gaurav’s suitcase.

George quietly went out but Gaurav made a teasing face to Aanya and ran, followed by an angry Aanya.

When everything was arranged in the hut, the two children spread out the note and scratched their heads.

> 23.5.12.12.9.14.7.20.15.14 8.21.20,
>
> 7.18.15.21.14.4 6.12.15.15.18,
>
> 23.15.15.4.5.14 16.1.14.5.12 9.14. 23.1.12.12
>
> 19.5.3.18.5.20 16.1.19.19.1.7.5 9.14 6.12.15.15.18
>
> 16.1.19.19.23.15.18.4 - AREA BOOM
>
> A.S

“This is similar to the note we made,” exclaimed a puzzled George to an equally puzzled Gaurav.

“Yes,” said Gaurav. “But what does it mean? And we know that it is from Dr. Abhishek, due to his initials A.S. But what does area Boom mean?”

George said, “This note is about the location of the chemical, as it will blast some area. And maybe the two women were Dr. Demon's wife and sister, as we know that they are in the plot too. Also, they are not caught, so they might have disguised themselves."

Gaurav said, "All I could make out while they gave the note in darkness was that they both had a dragon tattoo on their hands. Maybe all people helping Dr. demon have it too."

George clapped Gaurav on his back and said, "Well done, Gaurav!"

They continued discussing among themselves but could deduce nothing more. "Let's have a game of Uno," said Gaurav at last.

Meanwhile, at the farmhouse, Hardik and Aanya were thinking the same. Hardik was getting more and more doubtful. He thought if George was really speaking the truth. But Aanya was firmly convinced that he was not. "If he can trick me eight times without me suspecting a water balloon attack, then can't he trick us with a false note just two times?"

"Let's have a game of ball with Fluffy," said Hardik, at last. "I'm extremely confused to decide if George is speaking the truth or no." So, George and Gaurav were busy dealing and playing Uno cards, while Hardik and Aanya were giving Fluffy all different types of catches.

Before lunch time, snack time, and dinner time, Gaurav flew a plane to Aanya telling her to bring their share of food to them, as they didn't want to eat with her and Hardik.

The whole day was spent very lazily. The two boys at the hut played Uno, and tried to figure out the meaning of the note. Whereas, the two children at the farmhouse played with Fluffy all day.

Finally, at night, Hardik got a bright idea. He told Aanya, "Remember, what happened in the movie? The detective got a note from the thief, in which only numbers were there. Like number 1 represented letter C as 'one' has three letters and the third letter of the alphabet is C. And 1+1 is three + three, which is F, the sixth letter."

However, Aanya was firm about her belief of George tricking them, and hence didn't pay attention. So, Hardik insisted to take George's and Gaurav's dinner himself.

When George took the tray, Hardik said, "I'm sorry that I didn't believe you this morning, but now I think that you really aren't tricking us. Moreover, I have an idea to decode the numbers."

George smiled and said, "Thank you for believing me. But, I suppose Aanya has still not believed us, and I don't want to make things complicated for you. The workers are expected tomorrow after lunch. So, we will return immediately after breakfast."

Hardik nodded and went back.

Chapter 10

A Shock for George and Gaurav

"The pasta was super," said George. "But it was full of cheese. Let's have a run around the farm."

Gaurav nodded and they both began to run. As they went near the tents, they saw the two campers talk with someone.

"Hide in the shadows," said George to Gaurav in a whisper. Gaurav nodded and they both crept behind the shadows of the two tents.

To their surprise, the men were talking to the two women who gave them the note. Soham said, "You never came only. We waited for hours in that hut."

But one woman said, "Don't be silly. You both wore ghost masks as told and scared us. Then we gave you the note and you took it."

The two campers were bewildered. "That means someone, who came to know our secret came and took the note," said Soham and Pratham nodded.

The women were shocked. "What will boss say?" Pratham replied, "Dr. Demon will be furious. We will have to catch the thief."

George and Gaurav, or 'the thieves', nodded to each other, and quietly ran from there to the cottage.

The two scratched their heads to decode the note till late night. Finally, they gave up and headed towards the staircase.

The floor was slippery, and hence Gaurav slipped. He slipped near a wall, and tried to take support of it. While doing so, he pushed a wooden panel, which looked smaller than the rest. To his surprise, the panel went inwards and he fell. A huge, grating noise followed it, and a part of the floor gave way to a door kind of board. Next to it was a button, and an arrow which pointed to it showed, 'Press it and say the password.'

George and Gaurav were too pleased for words. George pressed the button and spoke, "Area Boom." Immediately, the door opened and the two boys saw some stairs leading to an underground passage.

They squealed and shouted with delight. Without thinking twice, they ran down the stairs and into the passage.

At first, it was very narrow, but later on it widened up. The air smelled musty, and whatever they spoke echoed very loudly and clearly.

Once, in excitement, when George laughed like a demon, it echoed in such a way that anyone would think the passage was filled of demons. Poor Gaurav almost jumped out of his skin when he heard that.

Soon, the passage widened into a fully furnished cave. There were boxes, a bed, chairs, a table, a gas stove, oven, and what not. "Food, read George. "Costumes, cutlery, books. There are so many boxes here."

Gaurav opened a box labelled 'Costumes', and found wigs, masks, moustaches, etc. "Looks like he wanted to stay here before he got caught, and buy necessities by disguising himself," said Gaurav.

George saw a box which was wrapped so tightly, that many men would be needed to open it. "Maybe it has the chemical," he guessed.

Gaurav said, "Look, the passage has ended. Let's go back to the farmhouse, wake up Hardik and Aanya, and call the police."

George nodded and they went to the door. "But how to open it?" asked Gaurav.

There was a button labelled, 'Press it and say the password'. George did the same, and the door opened. But to their shock, the floor of the hut was put into its normal position.

"We're trapped," said George. "Someone has undone the mechanism, and closed the passage. And I have a feeling that our dear campers came here in case they found something, and they found that the passage was open, and guessed that it was us. So, they closed it so that we don't tell anyone else."

Gaurav tried calling Hardik using his phone, but there was no network. "It's a good thing that we left the note under the water bottle. I don't think that the men will take it, as they found the passage and think all four are trapped. So, it all depends on Hardik and Aanya, if they manage to decode the note. Let's go to sleep, I'm tired."

So, the two boys slept on the bed, happy that it was comfortable, and managed to eat the food which was in the box. "Good thing I had a tin opener in my pocket," said George.

In the morning, after getting ready, Hardik told Aanya last night's conversation, and she too began to think that George was acting as if he was speaking the truth, for he never was so angry when they discovered his tricks.

So, while delivering the breakfast, Aanya decided to apologise to the two boys, but she found nobody there. "They might have gone for a walk," she thought and put the tray on the table and went away.

After breakfast, the two children and Fluffy began to watch the television. They soon got bored, as Fluffy proved to be very active and kept pawing at them as if he wanted to play. So, they went for a walk.

They soon passed by the tents, and the two campers stared at them in amazement. The two children were surprised, but said nothing.

They went to the hut, but were surprised to see the two boys still missing. They, instead, saw the note under the bottle. As Aanya picked up the note, the bottle fell with a thud.

The thud proved to be useful, as Gaurav and George were near the door of the passage. They guessed that it was Hardik and Aanya, so they shouted at the top of their voices. George went in the cave, got a steel plate and spoon, and banged hard with it.

Hardik and Aanya were startled at the sudden noise. Realising that it was coming from down, they were even more startled. But, Fluffy barked happily.

"What can it be?" cried Aanya. Hardik said, "Wait. Something is coming in my mind." After a pause he said, "George and Gaurav missing, George's suspicion about a secret way in the farmhouse, our doubt on the two campers about them doing something wrong, they getting a surprise on seeing us today morning, and Fluffy barking happily, this all indicates that George was right. There was a secret passage in the hut, and they both have found it. But Soham and Pratham have trapped them in and think we were in too. And now we have to decode this note and rescue both our friends."

Aanya gasped. "It is a good thing that we didn't believe them, or we too would have been trapped inside."

They went out, and heard the police siren. Inspector Aryan came out of the car and told them, "Your mother is unable to call the farmhouse telephone as well as George's mobile. She wanted to tell you that the workers are coming next Friday."

The two children thanked Inspector Aryan, and Fluffy woofed, but said nothing about their idea. As soon as the police went, the two went in the farmhouse and wrote all they knew on a piece of paper.

But the biggest clue was when the women told George, 'Wellington Hut.' Aanya's eyes brightened up. She said, "I think I understood it. The numbers connected by dots represent one word and the numbers represent letters. The word 'Wellington' has ten letters, and the first word in the note also has ten numbers. The word 'Hut' has three letters and the second word also has three numbers."

Chapter 11

Hunt for The Underground Passage

Hardik stared at Aanya in awe. Then his eyes brightened too.

23.5.12.12.9.14.7.20.15.14 8.21.20,
7.18.15.21.14.4 6.12.15.15.18,
23.15.15.4.5.14 16.1.14.5.12 9.14. 23.1.12.12
19.5.3.18.5.20 16.1.19.19.1.7.5 9.14 6.12.15.15.18
16.1.19.19.23.15.18.4 - AREA BOOM
A.S

"I bet you didn't think of this. In this note, no numbers are greater than 26. And there are 26 letters in total. So, can it mean that a number between one and twenty-six represents a letter. And there must be a list of that in Soham or Pratham's tent, which will show everything."

Aanya nodded. "So, we search their tents, which I would never dream of, if it hadn't been for the sake of George and Gaurav."

Suddenly, Fluffy began to growl. Someone was knocking the door. Hardik opened it and saw Soham, with his fake moustache. "The milkman gave your share of milk to us, so I've come to give it to you." Hardik said, "Thank you, but we don't want," and Soham went away.

Aanya suddenly said, "I think that you are wrong. Look at the note again. The 23rd letter of the alphabet is W, the 5th letter is E, the 12th letter is L, which is repeated twice. The 9th letter is I, the 14th letter is N, the 7th letter is G, the 20th letter is T, and in the same way, the 15th, 14th, 8th, 21st and 20th letters are O, N, H, U, T."

Hardik banged his hand on the table so loudly that Fluffy hid behind the sofa. Aanya comforted it and it came out again.

Hardik said, "The second line is 'GROUND FLOOR.' Hmm. Ground floor of Wellington Hut."

Aanya said, "The third line is 'WOODEN PANEL IN WALL.' Whatever does that mean?"

Hardik said, "The fourth line is

'SECRET PASSAGE IN FLOOR." So, if the passage starts from the floor, what is the meaning of the third line?"

Aanya said, "The fifth line is 'PASSWORD – AREA BOOM.' And then there are the initials of the scientist."

Hardik repeated everything in his mind again and then said, "Tonight, when everyone is asleep, we rescue George and Gaurav. Right now, we go and have a snoop in the hut. Check the batteries of your torch, and charge my mobile. We sleep early, after dinner, and wake up at 12."

Aanya nodded. She was too excited to even speak. But, much to the astonishment of Hardik, she ran inside George's room.

After a moment, she came out with a bag.

"It has George's water balloons. We might need it to protect ourselves from the men," she said. So, the two put as many of them as they could in their pockets.

Hardik went out and looked for Soham and Pratham. They were out, with shopping bags on their shoulders. He called Aanya and the two went in the hut.

Hardik said, "We have to press every wooden panel in the walls. One of them will open the passage from the floor."

Aanya nodded and the two spent half an hour pressing panels. "My palms are red," said Aanya, at last. "We seem to miss many panels."

Hardik said, "That's true." Then he suddenly stopped. "I say," he said. "I found the correct panel. Look at that. It is smaller than the others."

Aanya looked at the panel at which Hardik was pointing at. Yes, it indeed was smaller. She proceeded to press it, but Hardik stopped her. "I thought I heard some sound in the night, and it could be of the passage. We don't want to warn those two."

Aanya nodded and thought, "Just because of George's prank, I saw the men's real face. Just because of George's prank we didn't believe him and he went to stay in the hut. Just because of him, Hardik and I are safe and can try to rescue them."

Hardik ran towards the farmhouse but accidently stepped on Fluffy's tail. "He's been as good as gold that I didn't notice him half the times." So, the two ran to the farmhouse, only to find Mrs Sharma standing there. The two realised that it was lunch time, and happily took the food.

"I wonder if George and Gaurav have eaten anything," said Aanya. Hardik said, "They must have had something. Don't you worry about that."

Hardik was right. Down in the passage, the two boys were having a meal, but not as Hardik thought. They were having a great meal of chocolate cake, potato curry, roti. "Dr. Demon meant to have a great meal. I don't know how he preserved them, but it's good for us."

Hardik and Aanya were too excited to do anything, surprising Soham and Pratham, who guessed that they decoded the note and were going to rescue George and Gaurav in the night. So, they decided not to sleep in the night.

Chapter 12

Into the Passage – and a Shock

After having dinner, the two children slept, with an alarm of 12 am. The men, on the other end, ordered hot tea to keep themselves awake.

The alarm rang, and the two children awoke with a jump. They tiptoed out with Fluffy, who was delighted at the thought that they were going for a walk in the night, and the men saw them. Realising that the children were coming near their tents, they pretended to sleep.

Seeing them in bed, Hardik and Aanya relaxed and ran to the hut, with Soham Pratham following them.

As they reached the hut, they began to talk in their normal voices. "Here's the panel. Won't the men be wild to find George and Gaurav in the farmhouse?" they laughed to each other, not knowing that they would be wild, if they knew that the men were a little far only.

Hardik pressed the panel, and the passage opened. As he was going in, Pratham did the mistake of peeping through the window, for he wasn't contended with hearing. Fluffy heard him and barked, alerting the other two.

Aanya too felt this movement and heard the slight noise made by him. She stopped Hardik and said, "I think I heard some sound. Maybe those horrid men have come here too." Hardik didn't think so, but seeing Aanya's white face, he said, "Let's walk around the hut. If Soham and Pratham are nearby, we will spot them."

Soham glared at Pratham, and they ran back to their tents. However, Soham dropped his pen, on which his name was written. Not knowing about it, he ran.

Hardik was walking very fast, unlike Aanya, who was flashing her torch on every part of the ground. The light fell on a pen, and Aanya picked it. "SOHAM," she read and Fluffy barked.

She showed it to Hardik, who considered it, and after a moment, he spoke. "So, they have guessed about our idea, and came to lock us in too. But, you did a perfect job. Now listen, I'll shout, "There's no one. Let's go in," in such a way that those men can hear me. Then you shout yes and we both go in the hut. But, I'll go in the passage, and you hide somewhere. Then, the men will lock me in and go to sleep. Then, you free us and call the inspectors."

Aanya nodded, and the two did the same. Hardik and Fluffy went in, and Aanya searched for a hiding place. She chose to lie still on the staircase.

The men came, and undid the mechanism by pushing the panel even more. They were about to go but much to the shock of Aanya, Soham suggested, “Why not sleep in the comfortable beds?”

So, as they climbed up the staircase, Aanya didn’t even dare to breathe. But, unfortunately, Pratham stepped on Aanya’s leg and she screamed. But before she knew what was going on, she found herself thrown down the passage, her legs bleeding.

She shouted to Hardik, who was in the cave with the other two. Hardik gave them a surprise, and told his plan. Their joy knew no bounds, and they hugged him.

Then didn’t hear Aanya’s scream, but Fluffy heard and barked. So, they went to the door and saw her. George got a first aid kit, which he found in one of the boxes.

Hardik couldn’t believe it. “I’m surprised that he didn’t get a television here,” he said. But much to his surprise and amusement, George told him that he got a TV too. “He connected his wires to our cable, and enjoyed free electricity. No wonder our bill was double, and I was blamed for watching too much TV.”

Hardik chuckled, while Fluffy licked Aanya, and Gaurav covered her wound, and was quite proud that out of the four, only he knew it.

After Aanya felt better and could walk, she was carried to the bed. Everyone realised that they too were sleepy.

“It is a good think that there are four single beds. Dr. Demon must have planned one for him, one for his wife, one for his sister, and one as a daytime sofa,” said Hardik.

“No,” said Aanya. “One for a guest who comes to visit him. And there may be some gift for him or her too,” she said with a grin, and the boys laughed.

They switched off the night lamp, which stole electricity just like the TV did. They felt hot, and it was George who discovered the ceiling fan when he lied down on the bed, and its switch next to him. “Dr. Demon is crazy,” he thought, as he turned the fan on, expecting to see an air conditioner next, which he did see in his strange dreams.

Next morning, they all woke up at 8 o’ clock. “What will Mrs Sharma ask when she finds us missing?” asked Gaurav. “Oh, the men will tell her some cock and bull story,” said Hardik.

He was right. The men told her that they were still sleeping and would give them the breakfast. So, when the four went towards the door, they found four plates with a cup of milk, poha, and toasted bread. There were very few dog biscuits for Fluffy, which were evidently reduced by the men to trouble them.

After completing the breakfast, they left the tray there and knocked on the door loudly. The men heard it and took the tray.

In the cave, the four children discussed how to get out of the cave. "The men might arrange for a car in the night, and quietly steal the chemical while we're asleep, and leave a note for Mrs Sharma that we are trapped in the passage," said Gaurav, and the three nodded.

"Possible," said Hardik. "In fact, this is going to happen. But Fluffy will warn us when they come and we will launch a water balloon attack," and removed all the balloons he and Aanya had got from George's room.

George grinned and said, "At last my water balloons will be useful for us." Then his eyes widened and he said, "A passage starts from somewhere and ends somewhere. But there is no way out here. It might have got blocked. Why don't we explore the passage?"

Chapter 13

An Excellent Idea

Everyone considered it as an excellent idea. "It makes me feel bad that we're trapped and have nothing to do. We might even find a way of escape. Dr. Demon could have cleverly hidden it, so that the person who discovered it van be locked by the men and the secret would be safe." said Aanya.

So, four children and a dog went to the door and started inspecting the ground and the walls.

Hardik said, "It would be better if we search individually. I will search from the door to this line," and he drew a line with a chalk, which had in his pocket. "Then Aanya will search from my line this line with Fluffy," and he drew another line. "Then George will search from Aanya's line to the cave, and Gaurav will search the cave. It makes the job easier and faster."

Everyone nodded and took their positions. Hardik inspected the door very carefully, and at times he even used his hand to scrape off dust and soil, in case there was some hidden button which would open the passage door from inside, but had no luck in the door. Then, he knocked on the walls and floor regularly, but nowhere it was hollow. He finally gave up, and he was the first one to do so.

Aanya's work was very easy, as she said, "A dog barks at anything different or strange, and since caves are solid, Fluffy will bark at the hollow part of the cave." However, since Fluffy barked and ran all over the cave, Aanya had to do all the knocking herself. However, she too found nothing.

George too had no luck. He knocked till his hands were red, but heard a solid sound.

Gaurav was also doing the same knocking, but didn't know how to recognise one. While knocking at the wall which was at the end of the passage, a hollow sound did come, but he didn't recognise, and the others didn't hear.

Tired, everyone met at the cave and discussed. Hardik said, "This is weird. A passage has to have an ending."

Everyone agreed. They heard a knocking from somewhere. "Those two men, to give us snacks," said George, and he was right. "Goodness knows what story they told Mrs Sharma. I hope that she gets suspicious at dinner and calls the police."

This was their last hope, and they felt very bored of the cavi-sh lifestyle. After snack, Gaurav suggested to explore the boxes in the caves, for if there was anything interesting, they could tell the police.

So, they spent half an hour searching boxes. They found nothing useful, except a ball. "We'll play with it, to pass time," said Hardik and the others nodded.

However, Fluffy was a big nuisance. Before anyone could catch the ball, he would leap and catch the ball in his mouth and give it to Aanya. She would again throw the ball to the boys, and Fluffy would again catch it and give it to Aanya.

Fed up by this, Gaurav ran towards Aanya, snatched the ball, and threw it so fast that Fluffy couldn't catch. The ball hit the wall of the cave, and a hollow sound came.

Hardik, Aanya and George pricked their ears and stared at the wall. Aanya ran towards it and knocked it, and to their surprise, a hollow sound came from the wall.

Hardik turned to Gaurav, who was blank and asked him, "Didn't you knock this wall? It has a hollow sound, meaning there is more of this passage beyond it, and maybe its ending point too. If you had knocked it, we would be out in the sunshine now."

Gaurav realised that the wall gave a hollow sound and he didn't know it. He confessed, "I can't understand the difference between the two sounds. They sound similar to me."

But before anyone could get angry, George threw the ball and another wall, and it too gave the same hollow sound. "The sound is because of the ball."

But his doubt was cleared very early, as Fluffy began to bark loudly. Hardik switched his torch on and saw that Fluffy was barking at a rat, which ran towards the wall which gave the hollow sound first, climbed it, and went in a hole.

Hardik said, "The wall is hollow, and we need spades to clear it. I couldn't find any in the boxes I was searching. Did anyone find?"

George and Aanya shook their head, but George said, "I found four spades. I'll get them."

Chapter 14

A Way of Escape

Gaurav ran to his bed, opened the box kept there and said, “Come and get your spades yourself. They are too heavy for me to lift them.”

The three went and got their spades. “Increase your diet, kid,” said Hardik, and immediately dodged a punch from Gaurav. He hated being called a kid.

Gaurav and Aanya got tired in dragging their spades till the wall, so Hardik and George had to do the work alone, but occasionally being helped by Fluffy, who scraped some of the sand with his paws.

They two boys broke the roof fall, but had to clear the rocks. Panting, they reached the beds and told Gaurav and Aanya to clear it, for they were tired.

Aanya reluctantly got up, but Gaurav said, “My leg is aching.” The two boys understood his excuse, and looked at Aanya to hear another excuse. “My hand is paining,” she said, and went back to her bed, with a sleeping Fluffy under it.

Hardik and George sighed, and rested for a few minutes. Then, they went back, and after an hour of hard work, they cleared the roof fall. Both were perspiring, and jumped at their beds.

Looking at the clock, Gaurav said, "It is dinner time." There was a knock, indicating that the dinner was ready. Aanya said, "Our hands and legs are paining, so if you don't mind, please get our dinner too.

Hardik and George were red with anger and annoyance, but said nothing and got their dinner. After a good meal of vegetable nuggets and spinach parathas, and biscuits for Fluffy, Hardik said, "We go to bed and escape tomorrow *after breakfast* so that the men don't get suspicious when we don't eat breakfast."

Everyone nodded, and went to bed. "I hope that their imaginary 'leg' and 'hand' pain goes away tomorrow, otherwise we'll have to be prepared to carry everything, like a washer man's donkey," said Hardik to George. But since he already fell asleep with the hard work at the roof fall, Hardik too slept, and dreamt that he spent a whole day clearing roof falls.

Everyone woke up at 7 o' clock, and ate breakfast, with Fluffy enjoying his dog-food. Hardik placed the tray and knocked on the door, and watched the men take it. "Now for the escape," he said.

The four took all their belongings, and were about to go, but George took Aanya's bag, emptied all the balloons, and took out two gifts. "They have punching hands, and we might as well leave them for the men," he said, grinning all over his face.

Everyone voted it as a good idea, and set for the journey. As they passed the wall, the air became extremely musty, and were forced to wait for some time. When the air became better, they went in the passage. The rocks were uneven, and Hardik once tripped over them. "Better be careful," he said, his leg paining badly.

So, the others had to wait till he felt better. Then, continued their journey, walking carefully. The passage soon gave way to another wider passage. It was so cold that they shivered.

Soon, the cold passage ended and from it emerged a narrow passage, full of stalagmites and stalactites. At some places, they even joined, which made them look like a demon's tooth. Almost half the cave was full of them, and the ground ones were so many that it was tough to walk.

"I can't understand what grows from where," said Gaurav "It appears the same to me."

Hardik said, "Stalactites have a t, so they grow form top. Stalagmites have a g, so they grow from the ground."

"Yes," said George. "But funny finding them here. After all, Dr. Demon couldn't grow these, so it might have been a natural one he found accidently and made it its hiding place. But I doubt if he knew the cave beyond the roof fall."

"Might be," said Aanya. "Ouch, I've hurt my knee on this stalagmite."

The passage then ended, and Hardik shone his torch all around. No hole, no secret way, nothing. "Maybe it is a roof fall," said Hardik. "And we need spades to clear them, which are in the cave. And everyone will help."

So, it was decided that Gaurav and Aanya had to got all the way to the cave, and get four spades. So, unwillingly, the two got the spades and helped in clearing the roof fall. After half an hour of vigorous hard work, it was cleared. As the dust and soil settled, the four saw a long flight of stairs.

They climbed it, but were disappointed to see wooden floor over them. "Maybe this can be opened from outside too, and no one knows about it," said a mournful Aanya, and Fluffy woofed loudly, as if he was agreeing with her.

However, to their surprise, they heard a crating noise. The passage was opening! The children came out and were surprised to find themselves in the kitchen of farm 8, as Mrs Sharma was there, cooking.

"Hello children. I heard Fluffy barking and guessed that you'll were in this passage, which I accidently discovered while cleaning the walls. How did you go inside it?

Chapter 15

The Mystery is Solved

The four grinned and narrated the whole story to the astonished Mrs Sharma, who was gasping every now and then, praising them for their presence of mind and bravery.

“I thought that something was wrong. The men were very fidgety, and it is very rare that children are absent at meal times.”

Hardik said, “That chemical is very dangerous, and needs to be given to the police immediately. George, call the two inspectors and aunt. She might have called at the farmhouse, and no one picked the call. But tell that all is sorted. Gaurav, go all way to the passage door and lock it from inside. It is a green button, and I found it while exploring. Aanya, help in the cooking. We shall have a grand lunch. And I will quietly keep an eye on the men, and place our two gifts on the hut’s floor, when I get a chance. And make sure that the men don’t see you, at least till the police don’t come.”

Everyone nodded. Aanya, Fluffy and Mrs Sharma went in the kitchen. George called the inspectors, and was pleased go find that they were nearby and would reach in ten minutes.

Gaurav ran inside the passage, climbed down the stairs, dodged the stalagmites, treaded carefully in the cave of uneven rocks, and reached the door. He locked it, and ran at top speed, falling in the stones, and hurting his knee in the stalagmites. Then he came out, and closed the passage, only to find George putting the telephone receiver down.

The two went in the kitchen to help, but were sent out.

Meanwhile, Hardik was having a very tough time. He saw that the men were dozing, so placed the gifts in the hut. After five minutes, when he was firmly convinced that they wouldn't try to escape (though he didn't know why – they didn't hear about their escape), he went to Mrs Sharma's farm and was relieved to see the police van.

He ran to the smiling Inspector Aryan and Inspector Karan, and called everyone out. He poured out the whole story, starting from the false note prank to their escape. The inspectors asked Hardik to repeat almost every line, and wrote it in their police notebook.

When Hardik came to the part where the men locked them, Inspector Aryan and Inspector Karan became quite serious. "Being their first crime, we could have reduced their punishment, but as they locked you all in, they now suffer more," they said.

Mrs Sharma said, “Lunch is ready, so if I give them the lunch, they will go in the hut, and will find your gift. Then you can walk in and catch them red-handedly.”

Both the policemen approved this idea, and Mrs Sharma gave the lunch to the men, who said that the children were playing Uno. Then, they went in the hut and were surprised to find two gifts. Soham got a punch on his nose, and Pratham got a punch on his left eye.

They both immediately understood that the four had escaped, and tried to run too, but were stopped by the two inspectors.

“Good morning, criminals,” they said, and the men went pale.

“You win,” said they, and Inspector Aryan nodded, while Inspector Karan was handcuffing them. “Yes, we win,” he said.

The men gave a last glare to the children, and Inspector Aryan, who saw that, gave him a stern look. Then he smiled to the children and said, “Well done kids. You will surely get a reward.”

As soon as he spoke, a taxi came and out came Mrs Wellington. “George, your father is all right. They called me by mistake, and when I reached there, I thought of spending some time there, but I came here as soon as I got your call.”

The inspectors grinned and narrated the whole story, and Mrs Wellington was shocked. "Don't you dare to do anything dangerous in the future, she said.

Mrs Sharma said, "Lunch is ready," so everyone sat to eat lunch. After lunch, three police cars came, with the policemen wearing safety suits. Then, they went in the underground passage, and returned with the chemical. Then, in a highly guarded van, they took it to the laboratory from where it was stolen. Then, the scientists made the chemical ineffective, and disposed it safely.

Then, Inspector Aryan got a call, saying that the men spilled out the address of the wife and the sister of Dr. Abhishek, and they too were caught.

Then Hardik asked, "What is their crime?" "They helped the doctor in the robbery, and sent a message from him to the men," replied the inspectors. Then, when they went in their room, a bucket full of water fell on Aanya . "George!" she yelled. "You will never improve. Now no one can save you." And saying this, she chased George around the farm five times, till her anger died and repeated, "You will never improve."

***** THE END *****

www.ingramcontent.com/pod-product-compliance
Lightning Source LLC
LaVergne TN
LVHW091116150826
845673LV00002B/857

* 9 7 9 8 8 9 0 6 7 9 8 0 2 *